A Note to Parents and Teachers

Kids can imagine, kids can laugh and kids can learn to read with this exciting new series of first readers. Each book in the Kids Can Read series has been especially written, illustrated and designed for beginning readers. Funny, easy-to-read stories, appealing characters, and engaging illustrations make for books that kids will want to read over and over again.

To make selecting a book easy for kids, parents and teachers, the Kids Can Read series offers three levels based on different reading abilities:

Level 1: Kids Can Start to Read

Short stories, simple sentences, easy vocabulary, lots of repetition and visual clues for kids just beginning to read.

Level 2: Kids Can Read with Help

Longer stories, varied sentences, increased vocabulary, some repetition and visual clues for kids who have some reading skills, but may need a little help.

Level 3: Kids Can Read Alone

Longer, more complex stories and sentences, more challenging vocabulary, language play, minimal repetition and visual clues for kids who are reading by themselves.

With the Kids Can Read series, kids can enter a new and exciting world of reading!

Pup and Hound

For my mom and all our pups and hounds — S.H.

For Errol — L.H.

Kids Can Read ™ Kids Can Read is a trademark of Kids Can Press Ltd.

Text © 2004 Susan Hood
Illustrations © 2004 Linda Hendry

Kids Can Press acknowledges the financial support of the Government of Ontario, through the Ontario Media Development Corporation's Ontario Book Initiative; the Ontario Arts Council; the Canada Council for the Arts; and the Government of Canada, through the BPIDP, for our publishing activity.

Published in Canada by
Kids Can Press Ltd.
29 Birch Avenue
Toronto, ON M4V 1E2

Published in the U.S. by
Kids Can Press Ltd.
2250 Military Road
Tonawanda, NY 14150

www.kidscanpress.com

The artwork in this book was rendered in pencil crayons on a siena colored pastel paper.
The text is set in Bookman.

Edited by Tara Walker
Designed by Julia Naimska
Printed and bound in China by WKT Company Limited

The hardcover edition of this book is smyth sewn casebound.
The paperback edition of this book is limp sewn with a drawn-on cover.

CM 04 0 9 8 7 6 5 4 3 2 1
CM PA 04 0 9 8 7 6 5 4 3 2 1

National Library of Canada Cataloguing in Publication Data

Hood, Susan

 Pup and hound / Susan Hood ; illustrated by Linda Hendry.
(Kids Can read)

ISBN 1-55337-572-6 (bound). ISBN 1-55337-673-0 (pbk.)

1. Dogs — Juvenile fiction. I. Hendry, Linda II. Title. III.
Series: Kids Can read (Toronto, Ont.)

PZ7.H758Pu 2004   j813'.54   C2003-906689-4

Kids Can Press is a ʃʘⁿ∪s ™ Entertainment company

Pup and Hound

Written by Susan Hood

Illustrated by Linda Hendry

Kids Can Press

What was that?

What was that sound?

Hound looked around.

He sniffed the ground

until he found ...

... what made that sound!

It was small and round,

curled on the ground.

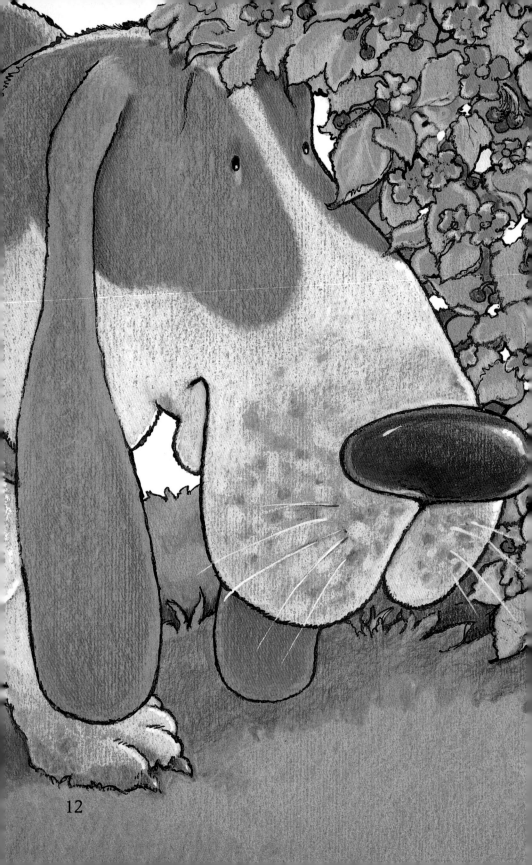

12

It was Pup.

He was fed up!

"Bow wow wow!"

said Pup to Hound.

"I want to eat —

now, now, now!"

Hound looked around

until he found ...

a stick!

Ick!

A shoe?

Ewww!

A bone?

Groan!

Then Hound found

a treat to eat.

Meat!

Neat!

Pup gobbled up

all the meat.

He left nothing

for poor Hound to eat!

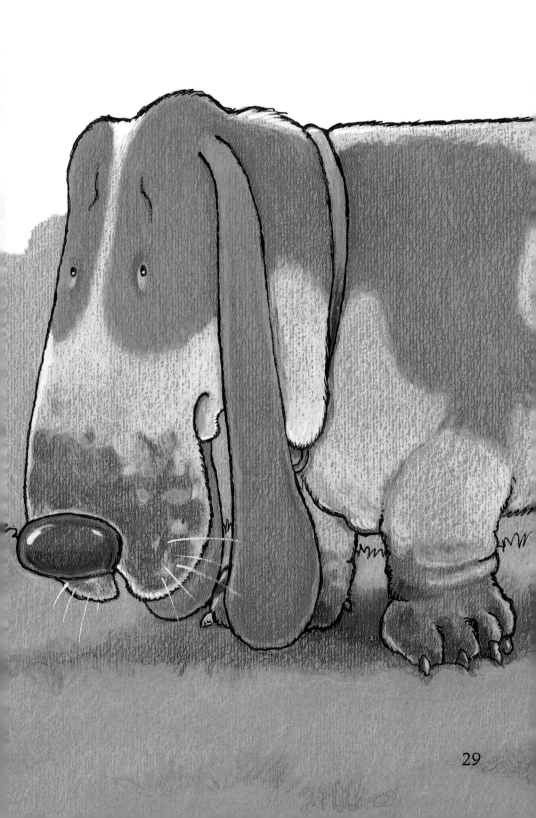

Never mind.

Hound chewed the stick.

Then Hound gave Pup

a good-night lick.